SPYMASTER

DEBORAH CHANCELLOR

A & C BLACK
AN IMPRINT OF BLOOMSBURY
LONDON   NEW DELHI   NEW YORK   SYDNEY

Contents

CHAPTER 1

Kit looked up, shielding his eyes from the bright winter sun. The bird was tiny now, just a small speck in the sky. It was soaring high above the timbered house and walled garden.

The boy felt numb. He had expected a rush of excitement, but instead he felt nothing. He pushed his unruly, dark hair out of his face and sighed. Who was he trying to get even with? You can't take revenge on a simple case of misfortune.

As Kit watched his master's hawk disappear from sight, the grim reality dawned on him. He had just made the biggest mistake of his life.

A cold wind picked up, and the gate of the hawk's cage swung open. From beyond the grave, the words of Kit's father echoed in his ears.

'These hawks are like children to Sir Francis,' he had said.

Kit's father had been showing him how to bind the wing of a wounded falcon. It was a warm August evening, towards the end of their last summer together. He spoke slowly, frowning with concentration as he trimmed the damaged feathers with a sharp knife. The bird was struggling to break free of his firm grasp.

'We must look after these birds well,' he had continued. 'If they ever come to any harm, we will pay for it dearly.'

Kit's eyes welled up with tears at the memory of his father. They had always been close, since the death of his mother when he was just a small child. She had died giving birth to Kit's little brother, John. Baby John had never thrived, and had been buried beside his mother a few months after his sad and bloody entry into the world.

Sir Francis had shown pity on his head falconer and taken Kit into his household, to be raised by a servant while his father continued working with the falcons. Kit had grown up knowing that he would take over from his father one day, and his apprenticeship had begun in earnest four years back, when he was ten years old.

Fortune had smiled on Kit and his father until a few weeks ago when an epidemic of sweating sickness hit the city of London. The fatal fever struck Kit's father down without warning. One day, he was at the top of his profession, a successful falconer for the Queen's Principal Secretary. The next day, he was dead.

Sir Francis sent a letter to Kit on the morning of his father's funeral. He could not speak to Kit in person, as he was away on the Queen's business. His brief message dealt a devastating blow. He had engaged the services of a new head falconer, who was due to take up his position at Walsingham's house in Seething Lane that very day. Arriving before Kit's father had even been laid to rest, this falconer was bringing his own apprentice to work with him.

Kit had lost everything in one fell swoop – his father, his family, his future. It soon became clear there was no place for Kit in Sir Francis Walsingham's household any more.

The grieving boy watched with mounting resentment as the new man took over his father's rooms in Walsingham's town house. He had been obliged to bow to the falconer when they first met. But he knew that he could not work for this man, a constant reminder of his father, so cruelly snatched away from him. Kit would have to leave the house that he had always called his home.

Kit stood for a few minutes and stared at the cage door swinging in the wind. The red mist that had clouded his judgement began to lift. In a fit of anger he had set the master's prize hawk free – he might as well have stolen it. The law was clear when it came to theft of any sort, let alone theft of such valuable property. If Kit was lucky, he would have his right hand cut off. But it was far more likely that he would be carted outside the city walls to Tyburn, to be hanged like a common criminal.

A *common criminal*. The thought struck home, like an arrow hitting its mark.

In God's name, what have I done? Kit asked himself, in shock. He had always refused to go with friends to watch public executions; death frightened him and he felt it should be a private affair, not an entertainment for bloodthirsty crowds. Even in his worst nightmares, Kit had never dreamed that strangers would gather together to watch him step up to the gallows.

Kit's thoughts turned to his father – what would he have to say about all this? Kit didn't have to think too hard. His father would be turning in his freshly dug grave.

Kit's act of defiance had been triggered by a hot-headed refusal to accept his bad luck. But now, above all he must stay calm and think carefully. He had to do something to reverse his fortunes and save himself from the hangman's noose. Speed was of the essence. If he moved quickly he could gather a few belongings and leave the house before the falcon was missed and somebody raised the alarm.

Kit crept back down the gravel path, the small stones crunching noisily beneath his feet as he passed the empty flower beds. Sir Francis took pride in his tidy knot garden, and in summer these beds were vibrant with the brilliant yellow of sunflowers and marigolds. Now, in the middle of winter, the cold earth was devoid of colour.

Kit approached the house. With a stab of fear, he remembered that the smallest movement in the garden could be seen through the windows. He cursed the fashionable and expensive glass that showed off his master's status at the court of Queen Elizabeth. The wooden shutters of a poorer house would have hidden his crime – but here in this wealthy household, he had acted in plain sight.

'Wait there!' A stern voice stopped Kit in his tracks. An upstairs window opened wide, flashing the sun's brightness a hundred times over in the small, diamond-shaped panes of glass. Kit blinked, dazzled for a moment by the light. Sir Francis Walsingham, one of the most powerful men in the country, was standing at the window.

Was he working at his desk, or has he been watching me all along? Kit wondered, his heart pounding in his chest. *Did he see what I have just done?*

Walsingham looked down on Kit from his vantage point.

'Come inside,' he said. 'I'll be waiting for you in my study.'

Like a condemned man, Kit walked slowly up to the house, entering through the servants' door and passing through the kitchen into the main hallway. He climbed the staircase, glancing up at the wooden linenfold panels that lined the walls from floor to ceiling. Sir Francis had the austere tastes of a Puritan, and his London town house had none of the ornate paintwork and gaudy tapestries that usually adorned the homes of the wealthy elite.

The master's study was at the back of the house on the first floor, overlooking the garden. Kit had never been inside this room before – Sir Francis used it for official, not domestic business. Usually it was kept under lock and key. Kit did not have to knock on the door. It opened as he approached, as though Sir Francis could see straight through the heavy oak.

The office was dark and gloomy – Sir Francis had shut the windows and drawn a thick velvet blind to blot out the winter sunshine. A roaring fire was burning in the hearth, casting a flickering light over the room. There were letters and official documents everywhere, piled up in corners and on the tops of cabinets.

Walsingham was sitting behind a large desk. He looked at Kit, waiting for him to speak first. Kit was convinced his master had seen the hawk fly away, so there was no point in avoiding the subject of its disappearance.

'It...it was an accident, Sir Francis!' he stammered. Walsingham narrowed his eyes, dismissing the lie. Frown lines creased his forehead. He stroked his neat black beard, which was beginning to show a few streaks of silver.

'We both know it was no such thing, Kit,' he said quietly. 'Fortunately, my hawk will return before the day is out, thanks to the fine training it received from your father.'

Walsingham's voice was even, giving nothing away. Was he angry, or strangely indifferent? Kit's fate hung in the balance, and the young apprentice was powerless to do anything about it.

'You must learn to control your emotions,' said Walsingham, standing up. He moved over to the fireplace to warm his hands. There was a chill in the air.

After a few moments' silence, Walsingham spoke again.

'Do you know what I do, Kit?' he asked.

'My father told me you are the Queen's closest advisor,' Kit replied. Walsingham looked closely at Kit, a trace of compassion softening his piercing blue eyes.

'Your father was an excellent falconer and a very good man,' he said. 'He was proud of you.'

Kit nodded, biting his lip and blinking back the tears, which were coming again.

'But your father did not know everything about me,' Walsingham continued. 'He did not know I am responsible for the Queen's security. I run a Secret Service to keep Her Majesty safe.'

He spoke slowly, as though Kit were a small child who needed to know right from wrong.

'England is crawling with Catholic traitors who want to kill our Queen, because she is a Protestant,' Walsingham explained. 'They want to place one of their own kind, a Catholic usurper, on the throne. I employ an army of secret agents to find out about these plots, so I can arrest the plotters.' He smiled grimly. 'Some call me the Queen's Spymaster, and not without cause. I have spies everywhere – not just in England, but all over Europe.'

A log shifted in the iron grate in the hearth, sending sparks up the blackened chimney.

Why is he telling me all this? wondered Kit.

It was as though the spymaster could read his thoughts.

'I am always looking for new recruits,' Walsingham said. 'Protestants with no family ties...in fact, young men just like you, Kit. Now listen to me. I will forget the crime you committed this afternoon, and you will not be punished as you so richly deserve, but only on one condition. You must agree to work for me.'

Kit's eyes widened with surprise. He was being asked to exchange his grim death sentence for a lifetime of service to the spymaster. Clearly, it was an offer he could not refuse. This cunning blackmail would guarantee Kit's loyalty by saving his life. From this moment on, whatever Sir Francis asked of Kit, he would have no choice but to obey.

Walsingham did not even wait for Kit to reply.

'You may stay in this house and tell people you are my falconer's apprentice,' he continued. 'But your true occupation will remain a closely guarded secret. You will swear your allegiance to the Crown and work for the Queen's Service.'

The fear that had gripped Kit was swept away by a huge wave of relief.

I'm not going to die! he said to himself, unsure whether to laugh or cry. Never had his life felt more precious than at this moment. He knelt down before Walsingham, clutching at the gold rings on his fingers.

'Thank you for sparing me, Sir Francis,' he said. 'I swear you will not regret your decision.'

Kit was surprised to find that he really meant these words; this was not a hollow promise, swiftly made and soon regretted. He vowed to himself that he would never let the spymaster down, whatever the cost.

CHAPTER 2

The sky turned blood red as the sun set on London. The December days were at their shortest, and although it was only four o'clock, darkness would soon fall over Walsingham's house in the city. Servants were busy lighting candles and tending fires, and preparation for the evening meal was well underway. Somewhere in the distance church bells began to ring out, warning law-abiding citizens that the night curfew was back in force. It was time for people to go home, lock their doors, and stay out of trouble.

But not for Kit. He put on the black, fur-lined cloak that Sir Francis had just given him, checking once again for the letter hidden in the lining. In all his life he had never possessed such a fine garment, nor been entrusted with such an important task.

'I want you to deliver this message for me,' Walsingham had told him an hour earlier as they sat together in his study. He passed Kit a letter secured with a red wax seal. Then he smiled, a barely perceptible twist of his thin lips.

'I am placing my trust in you, Kit,' he said. 'Prove yourself worthy of that honour.'

Walsingham reached for a cloak that was hanging over the edge of a chair.

'You will need this to keep warm,' he said, handing it to Kit. He showed him a pocket concealed in the hem.

'Hide the letter in here,' he said. 'And give it to my man tonight. He is expecting you.'

Kit knew better than to ask about the contents of the letter, or for the identity of its recipient. He stowed the letter away carefully.

'Where am I to find him?' he asked. Walsingham nodded approvingly, noticing Kit's discretion.

'He lives in the tall white house beside St Margaret's Church in Westminster,' he replied. 'Do you know where that is?'

Kit had lived in London all his life and knew every overcrowded street and stinking alley. This house in

Westminster was a long walk away, and the journey there would take him right across the city. But he knew he would find it easily.

'Yes, Sir Francis,' he replied confidently. 'You can rely on me.'

Walsingham looked thoughtful.

'I have been watching you over the years, Kit,' he said. 'You are loyal, just like your father was. Persistent and determined too. You need all these qualities to work for me. But you will also have to grow eyes in the back of your head. Take my advice, young man. If you are followed tonight, don't look over your shoulder and don't try to run. Find a crowded place to hide.'

He patted Kit's shoulder as he got up from his chair.

'God be with you,' he murmured. He went over to his desk and picked up a document from the top of a pile. He scowled as he scanned its contents.

'I have an urgent matter to attend to now,' he said, turning away from Kit and dismissing him with a flick of his hand. Kit took the cloak and slipped out of the room.

Kit left through the servants' door at the back of the house, as the sun sank below the rooftops. A narrow path took him behind the garden to the south end of Seething Lane. The temperature had dropped, and frost was already forming on the ground beneath his feet. It was going to be a bitterly cold night. Kit's teeth were chattering; he couldn't tell if he was shivering from cold or fear. He felt his father's dagger pressing at his hip under his warm, black cloak. Never had he felt more need of a weapon than tonight.

A few streets to the east, the tall turrets of the Tower of London rose above the city. Even as night fell Kit was aware of the Tower's imposing presence. As he set off on his way, he looked back towards the Tower – the final destination for many a traitor. Kit shuddered. He wondered whether the letter he was carrying would send some poor soul to that place, but he pushed the thought from his mind.

The streets around Seething Lane were quiet, and Kit only encountered a few men returning from an afternoon spent south of the river. From their high spirits, it looked like they had won some money at the bear baiting in Southwark.

Kit kept out of their way, trying to remain invisible as he walked in the dark shadows cast by the overhanging houses.

As Kit approached the river, the city seemed to spring to life. The late arrival of a trading ship at Three Cranes Wharf had kept sailors and dockhands working beyond the curfew, and crates of spices were being winched by torchlight from the deck of the boat. Kit walked a short way along the busy dock then stopped to watch the activity for a few moments. Some footsteps behind him also came to a halt.

Kit quickened his pace as he continued along the riverbank. Behind him, the footsteps echoed again on the uneven paving. Kit knew something was wrong. Trying not to look back over his shoulder, he took a sharp turn away from the river and walked up into a side street, where he knew there was a tavern.

Find a crowded place to hide. Sir Francis' advice was still fresh in his mind.

As luck would have it, a noisy crowd had gathered outside the tavern. Kit elbowed his way to the front of the group to see what the excitement was about. Two sailors had begun a fight over a barmaid, and punches were now being thrown.

The onlookers were picking sides and cheering on their favourite.

Kit watched the fight for a while, mingling with the crowd. Slowly, he edged towards the tavern and moved inside. The mood in here was calmer, but wasn't much quieter. Beer was flowing freely, double beer, which was twice as strong as anything Kit was used to. He paid a penny for a quart, and sat down with a group of men who were playing cards. They were too drunk to notice Kit's arrival, and they let him take a hand in the next round. Kit played well, but in his sober state he was careful not to cause offence by winning. He was also careful not to touch his beer.

I *need a clear head*, he thought, knocking his pewter tankard to the ground with a deliberately clumsy sweep of his hand. Its murky contents spilled over the filthy sawdust. Two long hours and many card games later, Kit's companions staggered up to leave. Kit followed them out of the tavern, past the scene of the brawl. The crowd had long since dispersed, and the street was quiet. Kit bid the men farewell and set off again. With huge relief, he realised that he had given his pursuer the slip.

I can do this, he thought. *I just need to believe in myself.*

Kit made his way along Thames Street towards Blackfriars, then headed north for St Paul's, the great church with a tall spire at the heart of the city. The temperature had dropped to well below freezing, and ice was forming in the muddy ruts left by the wheels of carts and carriages. Turning west again, Kit left the city through the old stone archway at Ludgate. He continued his westward journey along Fleet Street, then along the Strand, a broad, well-kept street with huge mansions that faced the river. When he walked past Queen Eleanor's Cross at Charing Cross, he knew he had almost reached his destination. He slipped through the gatehouse to enter the village of Westminster.

Taking a short cut through St Margaret's churchyard, Kit arrived at the white house next to the church. The full moon was directly behind the tall building, giving its outline a kind of ghostly aura. Kit took a deep breath, trying to steady his ragged nerves.

A blood-curdling scream split the air. Kit's heart skipped a beat – had he stumbled upon a murderer in the churchyard? But the scream was coming from the cellar of the big house in front of him. It was followed by the sound of stifled sobbing.

Kit gathered every ounce of his courage and walked up to the front door. He felt in the dark for the heavy iron knocker, and rapped it twice against the smooth wood. There was another silence, which seemed to go on for an eternity. Then a small grid in the door slid open.

'State your business,' growled a man's voice. It was a voice of authority, and could not possibly belong to a servant. Kit leaned towards the grid, not wanting to speak loudly for fear of being overheard.

'I am on the Queen's business, sir,' he said quietly. 'Sir Francis Walsingham has sent me.'

The grid slammed shut, and the heavy door opened just wide enough to let Kit through. The hallway was ablaze with candlelight. Kit's eyes adjusted slowly to the glare. With a shock, he realised he had seen the man behind the door once before. He was unusually tall and stood with hunched shoulders. A scar ran down the length of his left cheek, giving his smooth, clean-shaven face a strangely lopsided appearance. A year ago, this man had visited Sir Francis at Seething Lane. Kit's father had pointed him out.

'That's Richard Topcliffe,' he had said in hushed tones. 'He's a priest finder, and hunts Catholics down like vermin. Rumour has it that he tortures them in his own home, to make them confess to treason.'

The man was wearing a long apron over his fine clothes. The apron was dirty and spattered with something that looked like blood. Topcliffe wiped his hands before taking Walsingham's letter from Kit. He reached in the deep pocket of his apron to pull out another sealed letter.

'Give this to your master with my compliments,' he said.

Feeling sick, Kit bowed and turned to leave. Topcliffe opened the door again for him, but this time he barred the way.

'It was a pleasure to meet you,' he said, with a menacing grin. 'Any friend of Sir Francis is a friend of mine.'

Kit nodded, too frightened to reply. Topcliffe let him out of the house into the icy night.

CHAPTER 3

Kit ran as fast as he could out of the churchyard and down towards the river. A few small rowing boats were waiting at Westminster steps, ready to take their last passengers back to the city. Kit thrust a coin into the hand of the first boatman he saw.

'Take me to Old Swan Stairs, by London Bridge,' he said, gasping for breath. This landing stage was not too far from Seething Lane, and the river journey would be faster than the long walk back across the city. Kit could only think of returning as soon as possible to the relative security of his master's house.

Kit stepped down quickly into the boat, forgetting to watch his balance. He lurched wildly to one side, almost capsizing the boat. Ice-cold water lapped over the side into the hull.

'Take care,' snapped the boatman, clearly irritated. He reached down with a leather bucket to bail out the water. Flustered, Kit sat down on the cushioned seat, which was now soaking wet. He held up his cloak to protect the letter hidden in its hem.

'Forgive me,' he said. 'I am in a hurry – I have an important appointment to keep tonight.'

As the wherry edged out into the open water, Kit looked back towards the riverbank. The Palace of Westminster was lit up by the moon, which had now risen high in the night sky. Just to its right was St Margaret's Church and Topcliffe's house.

I hope I never lay eyes on that brute again, Kit thought with a shudder.

The boatsman was still angry with Kit and rowed silently, refusing to gossip in the way that usually passed the time with his passengers. For his part, Kit was relieved to be left to his own thoughts, and not to have to make small talk. He looked out over the Thames. The boatsman was rowing with the tide, which was fortunate, as it was speeding his progress.

Even at this late hour, there were many boats out on the river. The torches lighting their way were reflected on the inky black water, like a distorted image of the stars above.

Kit's world was unsteady and shifting, like the lights on the river. He could only be sure of one thing.

Sir Francis wanted to give me a warning tonight, he said to himself. *That is why he sent me to see Topcliffe. There is no turning back now. Once you're in the Service, there is no return.*

When the wherry pulled in at Old Swan Stairs, Kit paid the boatman a generous tip. The man muttered his thanks as he put the silver coin in the purse around his neck.

'This boat's my livelihood,' he said, by way of apology for his bad mood. 'If she sinks, I might as well go down with her.'

Kit understood exactly what he meant. From now on, he only had to make one false move and he was done for too.

Kit got carefully out of the boat and climbed the slippery wooden steps onto the riverbank. He walked along the Thames towards the great stone bridge, the city's one and only crossing over this wide, fast-flowing river. Feeling calmer now, he no longer felt the need to run, and in any case, this would draw attention to himself, something he wanted to avoid at all costs. He was grateful once again for his cloak; its lining was still dry and Topcliffe's letter had come to no harm. Kit knew that he would have to deliver it to Walsingham that night – he couldn't wait until morning.

Walking quickly, Kit turned left into the narrow streets that led him back to Seething Lane. He looked up at the moon and tried to guess the time. Dinner at Seething Lane would have been served and cleared away by now, and the household would be retiring to bed. Not so for Sir Francis, who always worked on his papers into the small hours. It was time to seek him out.

Kit returned to the house by the same way he'd left it, so as not to alert the head steward of his lengthy absence, and arouse suspicion among the servants. As he crept back through the garden he glanced up at his master's window. The blind was only half drawn and Kit could just make out the silhouette of Sir Francis, sitting at his desk in the candlelight.

He is waiting for me, thought Kit, with a strange mixture of fear and pride. He felt for Topcliffe's letter, wondering what its contents could possibly contain.

Once again, the door of Walsingham's study opened before Kit had a chance to knock. Sir Francis ushered him inside and quietly closed the door.

'Sit down, Kit,' he said, pulling up a chair before the hearth. The embers in the grate were glowing and the leaping flames of earlier that afternoon had died away. But the study was still warm compared to the bitter winter night outside.

Kit took off his cloak and sank down into the chair. Sir Francis was watching Kit like one of his hawks. Feeling uncomfortable under his scrutiny, Kit gave a nervous cough. Would the spymaster be pleased with the efforts of his new recruit? Kit had tried his best, but would that be good enough?

Sir Francis went to fetch two fine crystal glasses, and filled them with wine from a decanter. He offered one of the glasses to Kit.

'Have a sip of this,' Walsingham said, raising his glass in a celebratory gesture. 'You deserve a reward.'

Kit took a big gulp of the sweetened wine and

it slipped down his throat like honey. Sir Francis was still watching him closely.

'First of all, let me congratulate you for shaking off my man this evening,' he said.

So, all that business by Three Cranes Wharf was a test set by Sir Francis himself, Kit thought. He sighed wearily. Why wasn't that a surprise?

'Thank you, Sir Francis,' he said.

'You will go far in the Service if you outwit your enemy every time,' said Walsingham. 'Now, have you got something for me?'

Kit handed him Topcliffe's letter. Walsingham unfolded it and looked at it quickly. He went over to his desk and picked up a piece of paper. It was punched all over with a pattern of small holes. The spymaster passed the letter back to Kit.

'Read what it says,' he said. Kit scanned the first few lines of the spidery writing.

'It's about a new play at the theatre in Shoreditch,' he said, confused. What was so special about this letter? It looked ordinary enough.

Walsingham took back the letter, and laid it down on the desk, placing the paper with holes over the top.

'Now what does it say?' he asked.

Kit came over to the desk, and traced his finger over the holes of the paper. Each hole revealed a different letter. Slowly, he joined the letters together, and another message became clear.

'It gives the name of a rebel Catholic,' said Kit. 'A man called Anthony Babington. It says he is plotting against the Queen.'

The spymaster frowned.

'Topcliffe is right, he deserves to hang,' he muttered under his breath. He looked at Kit.

'The letters you carry for me will all be written in code. Some, like this one, will seem innocent enough, but will hide another much more serious message. Other codes will be a series of numbers, letters and symbols, which can only be understood if you use a key.'

Kit was curious. 'Who invents the codes?' he asked.

'I have many people working for me,' replied the spymaster. 'Some make codes, others break them. Perhaps you'll learn the art of writing codes one day. You're quick-witted enough.'

Flattered, Kit dared to ask the question that really bothered him.

'Your man in Westminster was not alone when I called on him,' he said. He didn't want to admit he knew Topcliffe's name. 'What happens to people who are sent to see him?'

Walsingham looked thoughtful.

'If they have betrayed the Queen, they confess to treason,' he answered. 'My friend is good at making them talk. And as you know, a traitor's end is never a pretty one.'

Kit tried to hide his reaction, but Walsingham saw everything.

'Don't be shocked,' he said. 'You must remember – if Queen Elizabeth is killed, there will be riots on the streets of England. The fragile peace we have all come to enjoy will be shattered.'

Walsingham began pacing around the room, the tension etched on his face.

'I have reason to believe that there is a new and deadly conspiracy, which must be stopped at all costs,' he continued. 'Elizabeth's cousin, Mary Queen of Scots, is at the heart of it. She is a Catholic, and many of our enemies would like to see her on the throne. Even though Mary is in prison, she is encouraging the plotters.'

He stopped abruptly and looked at Kit.

'The Scottish Queen must be destroyed, before it is too late,' he said.

'But, Sir Francis...' began Kit. He was interrupted by a knock at the door.

'It's time for you to go now,' said Walsingham. He opened the door to find his steward standing outside.

'You have a visitor, Sir Francis,' the steward said. 'A prisoner by the name of Gilbert Gifford.'

'I've been expecting him,' replied Walsingham. 'Bring him up here.'

As Kit walked down the stairs, he passed a young man on his way up, flanked on either side by two swarthy guards, armed with swords. The visitor had dark rings under his bloodshot eyes, and looked terrified. The door to the study opened and closed, and a key turned in the lock.

CHAPTER 4

Gilbert Gifford was only twenty-five years of age, but the events of the last few days had made this handsome young man look much older. For the past eight years he had lived in Italy and France, his Catholic faith making it too risky to remain in his homeland. Desperate to see a Catholic king or queen back on the throne of England, he had become part of the English Catholic resistance. Just four days ago, he had met with two leading dissidents in Paris, who had given him an important mission.

'We want you to help us open up a channel of communication with Mary Queen of Scots,' they had told him. 'For this, you will have to travel back to England. Your work will be fraught with danger, as the royal spymaster, Sir Francis Walsingham, has agents everywhere. But with Mary's help, we can overthrow her rival, Queen Elizabeth.'

Gifford longed to return to England, and his homesickness overcame the caution that had kept him abroad for so long.

'Where is Mary now?' he asked. Gifford knew that since she had crossed the border from Scotland about seventeen years ago, she had been taken from castle to castle in England, under constant house arrest. Her very presence in the country was a threat to her Protestant cousin, Queen Elizabeth.

'She is about to be moved to Chartley Castle in Staffordshire,' one of the men said.

Gifford smiled.

'I know Chartley well,' he said. 'I grew up just a stone's throw from that place.'

'We chose you for your local knowledge,' the man replied. 'That, and your devotion to the Catholic faith.'

Gifford was easily flattered. 'So what exactly do you want me to do?' he asked.

'You must carry Mary's letters from Chartley to London, to deliver them to our agent in the city, a young Englishman called Anthony Babington.'

Gifford recognised that name – the Babingtons

were well-known English Catholics. He was not surprised to learn that one of the family had become an active insurgent.

'It's up to you to cover your tracks,' continued his friend. 'But you will have to watch your back – be very careful.'

Gifford left the meeting in excellent spirits, his youthful optimism flying high. He set off for England at once, riding his horse at a gallop and heading north for the French coast. The weather was fair for the time of year, and when Gifford reached the port of Boulogne, the waters of the English Channel were calm. The young man boarded the first boat he could find, a merchant ship bound for Rye in East Sussex.

The few hours of sleep that Gifford snatched during the crossing would have to last him for a while to come. As the ship dropped anchor in Rye harbour, Gifford spotted some armed guards standing by the harbour wall. Walsingham's men were waiting for him to step off the ship; the would-be spy didn't stand a chance of avoiding them.

Gifford's arrest was swift.

'Did you really think it would be that easy?'

smirked one of the guards, as he pressed a knife to the young man's throat. 'Your game is up before it has even started. You are coming with us to London, to explain yourself to Sir Francis Walsingham.'

'How did he even know about me?' Gifford exclaimed, his surprise briefly outweighing his fear. A guard laughed at his naïve confusion.

'You can't outsmart the spymaster,' he replied. 'He knows more about you than you probably do yourself. I'll wager one of your fancy French friends is his friend too, on the sly. Take a leaf out of Sir Francis' book – trust no one. It's always safer that way.'

It was useless to protest any further. Gifford was tied up and pushed into a horse-drawn coach, which then began the ride north to London. After several hours bumping over rocky tracks, the coach stopped at an inn to change horses. Gifford thought of trying to escape, but it was impossible; he was held all night long at the point of a sword. The coach set off again at dawn, travelling all day until it reached London late the following night.

By the time Gifford arrived at Walsingham's house in Seething Lane, he had had plenty of time to reflect on the serious trouble he was in. He had heard what happened to traitors in England – their brutal punishment was common knowledge all over Europe. Gifford knew about the heads on spikes that decorated London Bridge, a grim warning to all newcomers to the city. Was this the gruesome fate that awaited him?

Stumbling up the wooden staircase in Walsingham's house, Gifford passed a rather unkempt young servant. The boy stared at him, with a mixture of curiosity and pity in his large, brown eyes. Then he averted his gaze and hurried away down the steps.

Something about the dishevelled appearance of Gilbert Gifford made Kit want to find out more about him. Why was he here at this time of night? And what did Sir Francis want with him? It had to be something very important to warrant his master's attention at this late hour.

Guards were standing outside Walsingham's study, so Kit couldn't go back up the stairs to listen at the keyhole. Remembering the window in Walsingham's study, Kit decided to venture outside again. Had Sir Francis left the window open? It was possible, but Kit wasn't sure. He walked through the kitchen, taking care not to wake the maid snoring softly by the fireplace. He opened the door onto the garden, and a blast of freezing air almost took his breath away.

Kit crept around the back of the house, stopping under the only window that was still illuminated by candlelight. As luck would have it, Walsingham's window was indeed open. Thankful once again for his warm cloak, Kit wrapped it tightly around himself. He strained his ears to hear what was being said above his head. The conversation between Walsingham and Gifford carried well through the crisp December night.

'...You are no better than a traitor,' Walsingham was saying. 'I know you are working for Mary Queen of Scots.'

'I have never met her,' protested Gifford.

'Not yet, perhaps,' conceded Walsingham, 'But my sources tell me that you have come to this country to make contact with her.'

Gifford's denial came a fraction of a second too late.

'It's true, isn't it,' urged Walsingham. 'Just admit it.' His quiet voice had an edge as hard as steel.

'If you confess now, it will be better for you in the end,' he said.

There was a short pause, then Walsingham continued, his words now a mere whisper.

'I'm sure you'd rather tell me than take a trip to the Tower.'

Gifford began to whimper, like a child. Walsingham ignored him and continued.

'My good friend Richard Topcliffe has very little patience for renegades like you. If he shows you his box of torturer's tricks, you can say goodbye to your fine looks, young man.'

Kit couldn't see Gifford's face, but he sensed the prisoner's terror. The tension was unbearable.

'I beg you, Sir Francis, take pity on me,' Gifford cried, breaking down.

Walsingham did not say anything for a full minute. It was as though he was weighing up his options, but Kit knew he had already decided what to do. He was like a chess player, toying with his opponent before laying down his next piece.

'Your prayers are answered, Mr Gifford. For now at least,' Walsingham finally replied. 'I have other plans – I want you to start working for me. But your friends in Paris must never know you have switched your allegiance, and of course Mary must also remain in ignorance.'

He paused to let his words sink in.

'The Scottish Queen must carry on believing you are her spy, while all the time you are passing her secrets onto me, her greatest enemy.'

Kit waited anxiously for Gifford's response.

Will this poor man deny everything he has ever believed in to save his own skin? he wondered.

He was surprised how quickly the answer came.

'Thank you, Sir Francis!' Gifford whispered. 'I will do anything you say.'

He began to weep again.

'Control yourself,' Walsingham snapped. 'Now down to business. Tell me, do you know an English Catholic who goes by the name of Anthony Babington?'

Kit held his breath. That was the name in the coded letter he had carried for Walsingham that night. The pieces of the puzzle were slowly coming together. He listened intently for Gifford's answer to Walsingham's question.

There was another silence, while Gifford considered the fate of his fellow conspirator. Should he deny his connections with Babington, or betray him now to curry favour with Sir Francis?

The spymaster coughed impatiently. 'Well, have you heard of this man?' he asked. Gifford's reply left no room for doubt.

'Yes, Sir Francis,' he said. 'He's the ringleader of a new conspiracy against Queen Elizabeth, and he needs to make contact with Mary.'

Walsingham sighed. Kit could hear the satisfaction in the sound.

'That's better,' he said. 'We have got to the truth at last. The task I have for you is simple. You must help Mary communicate with this traitor – just as your French friends have already asked you to do.'

Gifford was quick to catch on. After all, his life depended on it.

'You mean, if Mary trusts me to carry her letters to Babington, I can pass those letters to you, before he sees them,' he said.

Walsingham raised an eyebrow. 'You are correct,'

he replied. 'I will find out what they are plotting, and then you can deliver the letters to Babington. Mary and Babington won't suspect a thing.'

'What about my contacts in Paris?' asked Gifford.

'Send them word of what you are doing, just don't mention my name,' said Walsingham. 'They will never guess you're working for me.'

'How shall I smuggle Mary's letters in and out of her prison?' asked Gifford.

'I have thought of that,' replied Walsingham. 'Next week, Mary is being moved to Chartley Castle, a godforsaken fortress in the county of Staffordshire. I have made contact with a brewer in the nearby town of Buxton, who supplies beer to Chartley.'

Gifford was puzzled – he couldn't understand where all this was going.

'My brewer has promised to deliver his beer to the castle in a special barrel, with a secret waterproof bung hole that is big enough to carry Mary's letters,' Walsingham explained. 'Don't worry Mr Gifford – we will arrange things so the Scottish Queen believes the brewer is working for her, not me.'

Kit had heard enough. It was clear that England was a snake pit, heaving with poisonous vipers. He dared not think what the future would hold for the plotters Gifford was about to betray, and for Mary, Queen of Scots.

Even though it was past midnight, Kit did not feel tired. He made his way down the garden path to the bird cages. The prize hawk was back on its perch, just as Walsingham had predicted it would be. Kit looked up at the clear night sky, at the bright stars twinkling in the heavens. He felt trapped in the small garden, hemmed in on all sides by tall brick walls.

That hawk is like me, thought Kit. *It can't escape. Walsingham will never let me go now, because I know too much.*

The frosty grass glistened in the moonlight. Chilled to the bone, Kit returned to the house.

CHAPTER 5

When Kit woke up late the next morning, the household servants were already busy with their morning chores. There was a knock at the door and one of the maids, a girl called Bess, walked in. She was about Kit's age, and they had grown up together since the death of Kit's mother ten years ago.

'Sir Francis wants to see you,' Bess said. She handed him a set of neatly folded clothes.

'These are for you.' She looked at Kit, her green eyes sparkling with their usual mischief. 'The master asked me to give them to you and to tell you to comb your hair. He doesn't want you looking like a scruffy stable boy.'

Kit laughed.

'Of course not,' he joked. 'I'm his favourite apprentice after all.'

'Aren't you the lucky one,' said Bess, tucking a stray blonde curl back into her linen cap. Kit pulled a face at her. He felt anything but lucky, but from now on he would have to put on a cheerful act in this house.

'Out you go then, Bess,' he said, shooing her away. 'I'd better get myself dressed.'

Feeling awkward and uncomfortable in his new clothes, Kit knocked on the door of Walsingham's study. As he walked into the room, he saw that Sir Francis had company. Two men were sitting by the fireside, one of whom Kit recognised straight away.

Gilbert Gifford was looking remarkably relaxed after the previous night's ordeal.

So much for that man's conscience, thought Kit. He must have slept like a baby last night.

Gifford was wearing smart new clothes, sporting a fashionable white ruff around his neck.

I suppose Sir Francis wants us both to look the part, Kit said to himself. Now he has recruited us for the Service.

The other man in the room was clearly not bothered about appearances. He looked like he had dressed in a hurry, paying no attention to the latest court fashions. His messy fair hair had not seen a comb for some time, and underneath this, his long face was ravaged by smallpox scars. He had a habit of pushing his small round glasses up his bony nose, peering through them with a rather bemused expression. Kit wondered what this strange-looking man could be doing in Walsingham's company.

Sir Francis was the first in the room to speak.

'Good morning Kit,' he said. 'Let me introduce you to my friends.' He gestured to his bespectacled visitor.

'This is Thomas Phelippes, the most brilliant codebreaker in the land,' he said. The man began to protest, but was silenced by Walsingham. 'Do not try to deny it.'

Walsingham turned to Gilbert Gifford, as the young man shifted uneasily in his seat.

'Now tell me, Kit, have you seen this gentleman before?' Walsingham asked. By now, Kit had worked out that his master always required absolute truth in response to his questions.

'Yes, Sir Francis, I have seen him,' he replied. 'But only briefly.'

The spymaster hadn't yet finished with Kit.

'Mr Gifford and I had an interesting discussion last night,' he continued. 'Have you any idea what we talked about?'

'I must admit, I did eavesdrop on your conversation a little,' Kit replied carefully.

'I know you did,' said Walsingham. 'I left my window open for your benefit. I wanted you to hear every word.'

Kit glanced at Gifford, who was staring intently at his shiny new boots. Again, honesty was Kit's only option.

'I believe Mr Gifford is one of your agents, Sir Francis,' Kit said. 'He's going to help you to break up a conspiracy against our Queen.'

'I couldn't have put it better myself,' said Walsingham. He picked up a bag of coins from his desk and threw it at Kit.

'Take this,' he said. 'It is payment in advance for your services. I need you to carry Mary's messages between Mr Gifford, Mr Phelippes and me.'

Kit put the bag away in his pocket. It was heavy, possibly containing more than a year's wages. The money for this work was impressive, but what exactly was it for? He was now in the pay of a secret organisation that entrapped and tortured people for what was supposed to be the greater good. Was this bag of silver a fair price for Kit's innocence?

Again, he felt cornered. There was no way out of the task that lay ahead.

'You will arrange to meet these gentlemen over the coming months,' Walsingham continued. 'Mr Gifford will give you Mary's letters, which you will pass to Mr Phelippes. When he has deciphered them, you will collect them and carry them back to me. You must use all your cunning to make sure our enemies do not discover the link between us.'

Kit bowed low before the spymaster.

'I am your loyal servant, Sir Francis,' he said.

With those words, the last remnants of Kit's freedom slipped out of reach.

—————

Snow fell heavily in the week between Christmas and New Year. Snow drifts piled high in the streets and parts of the River Thames froze solid. There was little for Kit to do until the thaw came. In the meantime, he kept himself occupied by working with Walsingham's hawks. Sir Francis had told his new falconer to let Kit come and go as he pleased.

'That boy is still in mourning for his father,' he had said. 'He needs time to himself. You are not to question where he goes, or when.'

With the spymaster's protection, Kit was now free to do as he liked at Seething Lane.

The deep snow began to melt in the second week of January, 1586. One morning, Kit was sweeping slush out of the bird cages when Bess ran down the garden path to speak with him, her dimpled cheeks flushed pink with cold.

'I have just met an acquaintance of yours at Billingsgate Market,' she said. 'He asked if I worked for Sir Francis, then he gave me a message for you.'

Kit stopped what he was doing.

'That must have been my new fencing teacher,' he said, thinking fast. 'He's from that part of town.'

Kit had taken up fencing to learn the art of self-defence, but he had no idea where his teacher lived. He could guess who had spoken to Bess that morning: it had to be Gilbert Gifford. Kit was furious at the thought. If Gifford involved anybody else in their scheme it could only put them all in danger

– including Bess. Suddenly he felt very protective of his childhood friend.

'The man didn't say his name,' said Bess. 'He just told me to tell you he'd be at St Paul's Churchyard on Sunday.'

'Thanks Bess,' Kit said. He stopped her as she turned to leave.

'Keep away from that man,' he urged. 'He's got a violent temper. If he ever talks to you again, just walk away.'

Bess looked offended.

'Don't worry, I can take care of myself,' she said. 'You don't have to protect me.'

But Kit wasn't so sure.

I might have to if you get caught up in Walsingham's little game, he thought to himself.

———— + ————

St Paul's Churchyard was a well-known meeting place in the city, where people met to do business and gossip, while the Bishop gave endless sermons from his outdoor pulpit. It took Kit a while to find Gifford, who was slouching in the shadows under one of the great stone arches.

'There you are at last,' Kit whispered to him.

Gifford handed Kit a leather-bound copy of the Bible, a popular new English translation. There was a letter hidden between its pages.

Kit nodded his thanks. He grabbed Gifford's arm to stop him from walking away.

'Next time you need to get in touch with me, leave my friends alone,' he whispered angrily. 'From now on, I will be here every Sunday at noon. You can meet me to hand over the letters or to arrange another rendez-vous somewhere else.'

Gifford shrugged.

'Anything you say, young man,' he replied sarcastically, moving off into the crowds.

As far as Kit could see, Gifford had an inflated opinion of himself and took unnecessary risks.

How could anyone trust this man? he thought. But everyone seemed to, including Walsingham.

I hope Sir Francis knows what he is doing, Kit said to himself.

In the months that followed, Kit's relationship with Gifford did not improve. They met only briefly and spoke very little to each other. However, things were different with Thomas Phelippes, Walsingham's code breaker. Kit would enter his house in Leadenhall Street through a secret entrance in the garden wall, and the two would talk for hours in Phelippes' study.

At first, Kit was a little shy of this unconventional man, who could hold whole sequences of numbers, letters and symbols in his head and crack the most stubborn of ciphers with a combination of hard work and sheer genius. But as the weeks passed, and Kit got to know Phelippes better, he realised this socially awkward man possessed a hidden sense of humour. He was an amazing mimic, able to impersonate anybody perfectly after a single meeting with them. He would make Kit laugh as he strode up and down proclaiming doom and gloom, his voice and whole manner identical to Sir Francis.

'You have to make light of this work, or it will kill you in the end,' Phelippes said to Kit one day.

'I worry about Sir Francis. He takes everything much too seriously.'

Kit thought for a moment.

'Sir Francis has often told me it's more dangerous to fear too little than too much,' he replied. 'He suspects everything and everybody – but that's how he gets results. It's also the reason why he can never relax in his work.'

The weeks ran into each other, and the winter months passed by. Sir Francis was often angry when he read the letters Kit brought him from Phelippes. Sometimes the correspondence between Mary, Queen of Scots and Anthony Babington would plunge him into a black mood.

'We still don't have proof that Mary approves of Babington's plot,' he explained one day. 'We know what Babington's men are up to – they intend to murder Elizabeth and help Mary escape, so she can be crowned Queen.'

Kit was perplexed. 'If you know all this, why don't you arrest the plotters now, before they put their plans into action?' he asked.

Walsingham sighed. 'It's not that simple,' he

replied. 'I must wait until Mary admits her part in the whole affair. If I round up Babington's men too soon, Mary's silence will save her life.'

'But how much time have you got?' asked Kit.

'I don't know,' Walsingham replied quietly. 'That's the problem.'

As Kit carried secret messages around the city, he was often followed by enemy agents – but thanks to a happy mix of skill, intuition and luck, he always managed to avoid being caught. But the young spy began to realise that the dangers he faced on the streets every night were nothing compared to the millstone of worry around his master's neck. Would Babington's men kill Queen Elizabeth before Mary was tricked into incriminating herself? England's fate was on a knife edge and the spymaster could only watch and wait.

One evening in April, Walsingham handed Kit his pay. Another bag of silver – Kit was hoarding the money under the floorboards in his room, not quite sure what to do with this unwanted wealth. A dark cloud hovered over the whole business, and no amount of money would make Kit feel any better about it. Mary was a crowned Queen, there was no arguing with that simple fact. She was doomed, no matter what she did – and it seemed to Kit that she had not actually done much harm to anybody.

Walsingham seemed to sense Kit's unease.

'You have proved yourself an asset to the Service over the last few months,' he said, in an attempt to reassure his servant. 'Never forget that the peace of this land is at stake in this affair. You have earned this money, so don't feel guilty. You deserve it.'

Spring turned to summer, and still no proof came of Mary's guilt. But then one warm July evening, Kit brought Walsingham a letter from Phelippes that changed everything. As the spymaster broke open the seal, a smile stole across his face.

'This is it!' he cried triumphantly, waving the letter in the air. 'At last, Mary has given Babington her permission to go ahead with his plans. This letter proves beyond all doubt she is a traitor.'

He handed Kit the letter. Kit noticed something at the top of the page.

'What's that?' he asked, pointing to a small drawing. Walsingham peered at it.

'It's a gallows,' he replied. 'Thomas Phelippes must have drawn this, to show me this letter is a death sentence for Mary.'

For once, Kit did not find Phelippes' dark sense of humour very funny.

'What will you do now, Sir Francis?' he asked.

'I'll add a postscript to this letter,' replied Walsingham. 'It will be forged in Mary's handwriting, of course. I'll ask Babington for a list of the plotters. When he replies with their names, I'll move in for the kill.'

CHAPTER 6

Kit was reluctant to give Gifford the letter that would seal Mary's fate. He knew it would brand the Scottish Queen a traitor, setting off a chain of events that would lead to her death. Gifford would pass this letter to Anthony Babington, whose reply would only confirm his guilt. Mary and her friends had all fallen into the trap so neatly set by Sir Francis, the great spymaster.

Kit and Gifford arranged to meet at the Beargarden in Southwark, agreeing that there was more security among a raucous crowd at the bear-baiting ring than on a quiet city street. Gifford's hand trembled as he took the letter from Kit.

'What's the matter?' asked Kit.

'I have had enough of all this,' Gifford replied, ashen faced.

Kit felt sorry for the double agent, but there was nothing he could do to help him.

'You must hand this letter to Babington,' Kit urged him. 'You have no choice.'

'I know,' said Gifford. 'But I have betrayed everyone, even myself.'

The silence that followed was hard to fill.

'Let's meet here again next week,' Kit said gently. 'You'll have Babington's reply by then.'

But Babington's response to Mary's letter never came. When Kit and Gifford met the following Sunday, Gifford had news of another development.

'The plotters went into hiding last night,' he whispered, as the pair mingled with the crowd outside the Beargarden. Kit looked at Gifford. There was a note of hope in his voice, which seemed to imply that even at this eleventh hour, he believed Babington and his men could escape from Walsingham's clutches.

'What happened?' Kit asked.

'Babington must have realised the game was up,' Gifford replied.

'But why did they run off like that?' Kit asked.

Gifford shook his head. 'Perhaps they lost their nerve,' he said. 'Anyway, I shouldn't think Sir Francis is very happy right now.'

Something about the satisfaction in Gifford's tone of voice made Kit suspicious. Had he tipped off the plotters? It was possible, but surely that would have been pointless; it was only a matter of time before Walsingham would catch up with Babington and his friends.

Back at Seething Lane, Sir Francis was indeed furious. He pounded the floors of his study, his footsteps resounding in the servant quarters below. Every night for the next fortnight, the candles at his desk burned low before they were snuffed out at dawn. The spymaster became haggard from lack of sleep. But then one sunny morning in August, Walsingham called for Kit.

Kit ran upstairs, his heart thumping fast. The two weeks since Babington's disappearance had been calm – there had been no more letters to carry, no more unpredictable dangers to avoid. But now, something must have happened to change all that.

The disorder in Walsingham's study was striking – the turmoil of his mind was mirrored in the chaotic state of his paperwork. Documents were strewn all over the floor, and Kit picked his way carefully between them towards the chair by the spymaster's desk. He sat down and waited for Sir Francis to speak.

'We've got them, Kit!' he cried. 'My men tracked Babington and his men down this morning.'

Kit didn't know whether to congratulate the hunter, or feel pity for his prey.

'Where were they?' he asked.

'Hiding in St John's Wood, two miles beyond Westminster,' Walsingham replied. 'They were dressed in rags and had dyed their faces with walnut juice, in a futile attempt at disguise.'

Kit could only imagine the terror of the fugitives in their last moments of freedom.

'Where are they now?' he asked.

'They are being taken to the Tower, at noon today. You should go down to the Bridge to watch them arrive at Traitor's Gate.'

'I'll do that, Sir Francis,' said Kit, wishing he could run a mile in the opposite direction. He bowed, and backed out of the room.

'Wait,' said Walsingham. 'I have something else to tell you. Our friend Gilbert Gifford disappeared a few days ago. My sources tell me he has returned to France.'

Kit was amazed at the spymaster's calm reaction to this turn of events.

'Will you let him go, just like that?' he asked. 'Surely, he'll go back to spying for the enemy?'

'No doubt he'll try,' replied Walsingham. 'But Gifford's undercover days are over – the Catholic resistance in Europe have washed their hands of him now they know of his links with me. He is probably in more danger from his Catholic friends than he is from us. They're welcome to give him the punishment he deserves for his treachery.'

Kit had to admit there was rough justice to this opinion. But once again, he felt sorry for Gifford, a friend and enemy of both sides in this bitter conflict.

'It's eleven o'clock,' Walsingham said, as the hour chimed out from a nearby church. 'If you leave now, you'll get a good view of Babington and his men.'

Kit left the house and walked slowly towards London Bridge. Always crowded with people, carts and herds of livestock, today this thoroughfare was busier than ever. Word had spread across the city that some traitors had been arrested, so many Londoners had made their way to the Bridge to catch a glimpse of the condemned men.

Kit elbowed his way to the front of the crowd, and waited for the two long rowing boats to appear, taking Babington and his men to the prisoners' entrance to the Tower. The men were bowed down both by the weight of their chains and the shame of this public humiliation. Traitor's Gate was opened to let them in, and the huge white fortress seemed to swallow them up.

'From what I hear, those monsters were plotting to murder the Queen,' said a woman standing near Kit.

'Then we've got some good executions to look forward to, my dear,' her husband replied, sounding pleased.

Sir Francis will have to make a brutal example of those poor men, thought Kit. *Queen Elizabeth and her people will expect nothing less.*

Walsingham spent the next couple of weeks preparing papers for the Babington trial, determined that the whole affair would pass off smoothly and swiftly. Once he had finished with the plotters, he could move onto his real target, Mary Queen of Scots.

'I need you to help Thomas Phelippes transcribe some letters and documents for the trial,' Walsingham told Kit. 'Phelippes has asked for your assistance.'

'I would be happy to help,' Kit replied. Unfortunately, backing out at this late stage was not an option.

The Babington trial took place in the middle of September, at the Palace of Westminster. As Kit had expected, the outcome was quick and decisive.

'They've all been sentenced to death,' the spymaster told Kit, on his return to Seething Lane that night. He looked relieved.

'Did the plotters put up much of a defence?' Kit asked.

'Some of them spoke well at the trial,' replied Walsingham. 'But they all knew it was hopeless.' He paused, and looked at Kit. 'The executions begin tomorrow.'

'Why so soon?' Kit asked, his blood running cold.

'Any delay would be dangerous,' explained Walsingham. 'I have persuaded the Queen that we need to move fast to maintain public order. She has accepted the fact that the punishment must be severe, to fit the gravity of the crime.'

Kit didn't want to think about the violent executions that he had helped to bring about.

'You must go along to watch, Kit,' Walsingham went on. 'I cannot attend myself – I must keep a low public profile at all times. But I would like you to give me an eyewitness account of the whole event.'

With a sinking heart, Kit left the house early the next morning. He made his way westwards out of the city, past Holborn towards St Giles in the Field. A huge crowd had already formed around a set of hastily constructed gallows. Kit lingered at the back, in no rush to find a good vantage point from which to view the executions. He watched as Babington's men were dragged on wooden hurdles to the site.

Suddenly, Kit felt a firm grip on his elbow, and found himself being propelled forwards through the crowd.

'Come with me,' said a familiar voice in his ear. 'I'll help you get a better view.'

Kit would know that voice anywhere; it belonged to Richard Topcliffe, Walsingham's cruel friend from the village of Westminster.

'Sir Francis told me I would find you here,' Topcliffe whispered.

'So we meet again,' replied Kit coldly. He shook himself free of Topcliffe's grasp and forced himself to turn round and look the torturer in the eye. 'Thank you for your kind offer,' he said, with as much bravado as he could muster. 'But I would rather keep my own company today.'

He darted into the crowd and ducked out of sight before Topcliffe could grab hold of him again.

Hiding behind a tree, Kit watched as the traitors were led up to the gallows. Their final speeches and prayers were drowned out by the jeering crowd. Ropes were placed around the men's necks and wooden boards were kicked away from under their feet. Before they choked to death, they were cut down from the gibbet and stripped of their clothes.

The bloodlust of the crowd became frenzied. A woman near Kit was holding up her child, so the small boy would not miss a moment of the gruesome spectacle.

'Tell me what you can see!' she cried.

'They've got their knives out now,' he replied, caught up in the hysteria. 'Death to the traitors!'

Kit watched in horror as one by one, the dying men were hacked apart. Their genitals were cut off and their guts were dug out of their bellies to be thrown on a fire. Finally, the men's still-beating hearts were gouged from their bodies. Kit turned away in disgust.

'Show us their heads,' bayed the crowd. With the plotters dead at last, their heads were chopped off and lifted up on spikes, for all to see. Kit could take no more. He doubled over and threw up on the ground.

Wiping vomit from his mouth, Kit began to run through the cheering crowd. Tears were streaming down his face.

I *must get away from here*, he repeated to himself, over and over again. He took no notice of where he was going, running for what seemed like miles. At last, he ended up on the reedy banks of the River Thames, not far from the Tower.

For many hours, Kit sat on the riverbank, staring at the tall ships passing by on the water.

'Oh God, show me a way out of this living hell,' he prayed.

The weak autumn sun sank in the sky.

If I run away, Sir Francis will hunt me down, he thought. *He can't let me out of his sight – unlike Gifford, I do not have useful enemies who will make me disappear.*

Kit stood up slowly and turned back towards Seething Lane. He had nowhere else to go.

CHAPTER 7

As Kit made his way back home, the first street parties were already underway. The curfew had been lifted that night, to allow people to celebrate the death of the traitors. Bells were ringing out from churches all across the city.

Kit walked past bonfires on street corners, where cheerful children and adults were gathered together, eating street food and dancing to the music of fiddles and pipes.

'God save Queen Elizabeth!' cried an old woman, addressing no one in particular. The taverns were spilling out onto the pavements, and everyone seemed happy for the excuse to eat, drink and be merry. Kit was in no mood to join them. As he reached Walsingham's house in Seething Lane, he met Bess on her way out with a group of servants.

As usual, she was curious about his comings and goings.

'Where have you been all day, Kit?' she asked. 'Have you heard what happened to those traitors?'

Kit nodded, and attempted a smile.

'They got what they deserved,' he said, knowing that was the answer she would expect. 'Actually, that's where I've been today.'

'At the executions?' cried Bess, impressed. 'They say it was a bloody affair. Come and tell us about it! Sir Francis has given us all the evening off, and that means you too, Kit.'

She peered at Kit, suddenly noticing his sickly pallor.

'Are you alright?' she asked. Kit shook his head.

'I don't feel like celebrating,' he replied.

'Was it really that bad?' she asked, frowning. But she couldn't wait any longer on the doorstep. 'I've got to go.' She whistled at her friends to make them stop for her.

'Get some rest,' she said, looking Kit up and down. 'You look like you need it.'

Then she ran off to catch up with her friends.

Kit stumbled into the house, expecting to be

summoned by Walsingham at any moment. But the spymaster was not at home – he had been called away to court. Kit went to his room and lay down on his bed, sinking almost instantly into an exhausted, dreamless sleep.

To Kit's enormous relief, Walsingham stayed away from Seething Lane for a whole week. Kit took the time to reflect on his predicament.

Perhaps things will quieten down now, he said to himself. *Sir Francis will be busy arranging the trial of the Scottish Queen, so I can slip into the background. God willing, the whole affair will be over in a matter of weeks. Things will go back to some kind of normality. Maybe I'll even be able to retire from the Service altogether...*

But this happy illusion was soon shattered when Walsingham returned to Seething Lane. He had been at the Palace of Westminster, trying to win the Queen's approval for his plans.

'God's Truth, she is an impossible woman!'

he exclaimed, as Kit entered his study. Walsingham had asked for chamomile tea, to soothe some shooting pains in his stomach.

Kit handed his master a steaming cup and Walsingham took a sip of the pale brown liquid.

'I need stronger stuff than this,' he said. He frowned at Kit, deciding whether to take him into his confidence before he was gripped by a painful spasm, which made him put down the cup. His decision appeared to be made.

'I had thought my biggest challenge would be to prove Mary's guilt,' he said quietly. 'But I have enough evidence to convict her a hundred times over. The problem is not Mary, it is Elizabeth.'

Kit frowned. 'Why is that so, Sir Francis?' he asked.

'Our Queen has re-discovered her finer sensibilities,' Walsingham explained. 'She doesn't want her cousin Mary to be treated like a commoner.' He scowled. 'She won't let Mary's trial take place at the Tower, and is using every delay tactic in the book. If Elizabeth has her way, Mary won't have a trial at all.'

Mary is her closest living relative, thought Kit. *She is next in line to the throne. Perhaps that is at the heart of all this*. But he kept that dangerous thought to himself.

'Well, Mary shall have a trial fit for royalty, if that is what it takes to keep Elizabeth happy,' Walsingham said through gritted teeth.

Over the next few days, the letters and messages began piling up in Walsingham's study. Kit was perfectly placed to act again as a courier for his master. Walsingham had picked out Fotheringhay Castle in Northamptonshire for the trial of Mary – just far enough out of London and away from the public eye to satisfy the anxious Elizabeth.

Mary was taken from Chartley Castle to Fotheringhay and preparations were made for the trial to take place there, a month after the executions of the Babington plotters. Kit followed the unfolding events with mixed feelings. On the one hand, he would much rather no more blood was shed. He had seen enough of that to last a lifetime at St Giles in the Field. But the only way Kit could imagine an end to his work for the Service was through the death of Mary, the focal point for all Catholic rebellion. Her destruction was probably the only thing that could set him free from the Service.

Mary's trial finally took place in October 1586. Thomas Phelippes was invited to attend, as his codebreaking evidence would be crucial to Mary's prosecution. Golden leaves were falling from the trees as Walsingham set off for Fotheringhay with Phelippes. Just before the pair left Seething Lane, Phelippes took Kit to one side for a quiet word.

'I don't think Queen Elizabeth will even show up at the trial,' he said.

'Poor Sir Francis,' Kit replied, biting his lip. The spymaster's frustration was easy to imagine.

'But that isn't the worst of it,' continued Phelippes. 'We can convict Mary in the Queen's absence. But only Elizabeth can sign Mary's death warrant – without her signature, all our work will be in vain. This whole trial will be a pointless farce.'

Walsingham returned to Seething Lane a week later. The trial at Chartley Castle had only lasted a couple of days. On his first evening back, the spymaster summoned Kit to his study. It was impossible to ignore the grim expression on his face.

'What happened?' Kit asked, fearing the worst. 'Was Mary found innocent?'

'Of course not,' Walsingham replied with a bitter laugh. 'She is guilty as sin. But now the Queen tells me she will not condemn Mary to death, despite the clear decision of her court. It is madness!'

So Phelippes was right after all, thought Kit. *Walsingham's schemes are teetering on the brink of collapse.*

'Doesn't the Queen want Mary to die?' Kit asked.

'Yes, but she is afraid,' replied Walsingham. 'She thinks that if Mary is executed, her Catholic enemies will attack England. We already know the King of Spain has a large fleet of ships, ready to set sail at any time.'

'Will there be an invasion?' Kit asked, fear rising in his throat at the thought.

Walsingham stroked his beard thoughtfully. 'If so, we will be ready,' he replied. 'The Service will make sure of that.'

Kit returned to the problem of Elizabeth.

'Is the Queen frightened of having her family's blood on her hands?' he asked.

'Perhaps,' replied Walsingham. 'But this is not just about the Queen's delicate feelings, it is about her basic survival. When I think of all the years I've spent trying to protect Her Majesty...and now she is throwing all my hard work back in my face!'

Walsingham sat down suddenly, white as chalk. He clutched his stomach and winced with pain.

'All this is making me ill,' he said. 'Believe me, Mary must have a public execution as soon as possible, to silence every Catholic rebel in the land.'

The stubborn will of Queen Elizabeth was pitted against the iron resolve of Sir Francis. For two long months, Elizabeth refused to bow to any pressure, but finally, Walsingham's persistence paid off. One icy December day, the Queen gave in and announced the death sentence on her cousin Mary. It was a year to the day since Kit had joined the Service. He felt about ten years older than the innocent young boy who had overheard that discussion between Sir Francis and

Gilbert Gifford, as he shivered with cold under the spymaster's window.

Two more months dragged by before Queen Elizabeth finally gave her signature to the death warrant in February 1587. The stress and tension took its toll on Walsingham. The night after the document was signed, Kit heard a loud crash coming from his master's study. He rushed upstairs to find Walsingham lying on the floor beside an upturned chair. He was drifting in and out of consciousness. Kit bent down to check his master's shallow breathing.

'Fetch my physician,' Walsingham murmured in Kit's ear.

By the time Kit returned with the doctor, Walsingham was as pale as death. The doctor loosened the sick man's clothing and gently felt his stomach.

'I'll give you something to ease your pain, Sir Francis,' he said. Kit could tell from the doctor's expression that Walsingham's condition was serious. He watched as the doctor gave Walsingham a few drops of poppy juice from a glass vial then turned to Kit.

'Sir Francis must rest,' he said, as he made Walsingham comfortable on the couch.

'Get him some blankets, and tend to this fire.'

The fire in the grate had burned out, and Kit suddenly realised how cold the room was.

'On no account should you let him get up and work,' the doctor warned. 'It would kill him.'

The following evening, Walsingham called Kit to his bedside. He was in a subdued mood, but the recent crisis seemed to have focussed his mind.

'We can't afford any more delay,' he said simply. 'I have been ordered to stay in bed for a fortnight – so I will simply have to rely on you and Phelippes. You must help him to make arrangements for Mary's execution. Whatever happens, Queen Elizabeth must hear nothing more of it until Mary is dead. I don't want to risk a last-minute royal pardon.'

Kit was speechless. Surely such huge responsibility should not rest, even partly, on his shoulders?

He was just a small cog in Walsingham's vast machine. But despite his weakness, the spymaster had not lost his knack of reading Kit's thoughts.

'Don't worry, Kit,' he said. 'It's not all down to you. Phelippes will tell you what to do. But the execution must happen quickly, involving as few of us as possible. Our Catholic enemies must hear nothing of it until the deed is done.'

Kit bowed. Once more he would have to obey Walsingham's orders against his better judgement.

'One more thing, Kit,' whispered the spymaster, his voice faint with the effort of speech. 'I want you to go to Fotheringhay Castle to witness Mary's execution for me. I must know beyond a shadow of a doubt that it has been carried out according to my instructions.'

Kit swallowed hard. It was the last thing in the world he wanted to do, but yet again, he had no choice.

CHAPTER 8

It was still dark when Kit saddled up his horse in Walsingham's stable. The torchlight cast eerie shadows on the walls, as the drowsy horses shifted among the bales of hay. Kit picked his favourite stallion, a Neapolitan called Borin. Walsingham owned many horses, and Borin had the most reliable temperament for the long and difficult journey ahead.

The seventy-five miles north to Fotheringhay Castle would take two full days, so Kit set off at first light. As he rode away from the house, he saw a figure standing in the doorway, waving at him to stop. It was his friend Bess.

'You'll need your cloak,' she called out to him. 'It's going to snow.'

The February morning was bitterly cold. Snow that had been in the air for a week had still not fallen

– and Bess was right, it would probably arrive today or tomorrow. Kit sighed with frustration, turning Borin around to trot back to the house.

'Thanks, Bess,' he said, taking the fur-lined cloak that Walsingham had given him. 'You are very good to me. You always seem to know what I need before I have worked it out for myself.'

Bess smiled. 'I'm just looking out for you,' she said, turning back into the house. 'Have a good trip, wherever you're going.'

Something in the tone of her voice implied that she already knew.

After a long day's ride, Kit arrived in Cambridge. He found a wayside inn and left Borin in the hands of a competent stable boy. The horse was exhausted.

'He'll need a good feed and a decent rest,' Kit instructed the boy as he went inside the inn.

Kit sat quietly with a tankard of beer and a hot pie, watching some university students playing a round of cards. His thoughts flew back to his first errand for Sir Francis, on that night over a year ago, which had sealed his future in the Service. Back then he had joined in with the drunken card game. But tonight he felt strangely detached, as though he were watching these students in a dream. The young men were not much older than Kit, but they were worlds apart from him in every other way. Overcome with loneliness, Kit left his uneaten meal and went upstairs to get some rest.

The following morning, Kit was the first traveller to leave the inn.

'Off somewhere exciting?' the stable boy asked as he led Borin out into the yard. Unable to think of a suitable reply, Kit nodded and gave the boy a coin for his trouble. Then he mounted his horse and set off at a brisk pace.

Kit made good progress, and that night he stopped at an inn not far from Fotheringhay. He arrived at the castle at dawn on 8th February 1587. The sun was rising in a pale pink sky, making frost sparkle on the fields like a veil of diamonds. Kit rode across the drawbridge, passing over the deep castle moat. There were a few east-facing windows in the old castle walls, and Kit hoped that the Scottish Queen was looking out of one of them. It would be the last sunrise she would ever see.

Kit showed his official papers, and was quickly admitted into the castle buildings. A guard took him straight to the Great Hall. Kit was one of the last of the invited guests to arrive – about three hundred people were already assembled in the large, draughty chamber. There was an uneasy silence, with much coughing and shuffling of feet as the people stood and waited. The execution was set for eight o'clock that morning. All eyes were fixed on the large wooden scaffold that had been erected in the middle of the hall. Tension mounted as the minutes passed. Then there was a commotion at the entrance.

'Here she comes at last,' whispered a man standing next to Kit. 'Look, she can hardly walk.'

Mary moved slowly into the room, supported on both sides by her ladies in waiting. She held her head up high, wisps of her long red hair falling over her shoulders. The time of incarceration had not been kind to Mary, and she looked older than her forty-five years. In the public imagination, she was still young and beautiful, an ambitious pretender to the throne. Kit was shocked at the reality before him – Mary was old, arthritic and walked with a limp.

'That's what comes of spending almost twenty years

under house arrest,' Kit said to his neighbour.

Mary was helped up onto the scaffold. She said some Catholic prayers in Latin, and then took off her black cloak. To Kit's surprise, she was wearing a scarlet dress underneath. The colour red was usually reserved for martyrs, so this was a political statement, a bold rallying cry to her supporters. Mary was telling the world she was about to die for her Catholic faith.

'Traitor!' an angry voice called out from the crowd.

One of Mary's ladies stepped forward to tie a white handkerchief over the Queen's eyes. Mary knelt down, showing remarkable courage as she laid her head carefully on the executioner's block. As the executioner raised his axe, Kit looked down at his feet. After the Babington bloodbath, he had no stomach for the scene that was to come. There was a swooshing sound as the axe swung through the air. It missed Mary's neck, striking the back of her head. The crowd gasped.

Kit's neighbour nudged him.

'Don't you want to see this with your own eyes?' he asked. 'Many folk would give their right hand to be here today.'

'I would gladly give mine to be anywhere else,' Kit replied grimly. But he forced himself to look up.

After two more deadly blows of the axe, the deed was finally done. The executioner lifted Mary's head up to show the people, and there was a sickening thud as it fell to the floor, leaving a red wig dangling in the executioner's hands. The scene unfolding before Kit was the stuff of nightmares.

'Can you see her lips?' asked Kit's neighbour, gawping at the decapitated head on the ground.

Mary's lips were still moving.

'It looks like she's praying,' said Kit.

A stunned silence was broken by the unexpected sound of barking. A small lapdog was pulled from under Mary' skirts. The terrified pet was covered in the blood of its mistress.

'Take that animal away,' ordered the executioner. 'And prepare the body for burial.'

Kit turned to his neighbour.

'What happens now?' he asked.

'Her clothes will be burnt, so the Catholics can't turn them into relics,' the man answered. 'Then her body will be buried inside these castle walls.'

Kit shook his head.

'Not much of a royal farewell,' he muttered under his breath. His thoughts turned to Queen Elizabeth, and he wondered how she would react to the news of her cousin's death. For himself, he had seen enough executions to last a lifetime.

On his journey back to London that afternoon, Kit felt numb. Nothing seemed to make any sense.

How can Sir Francis be so sure he is right? he asked himself. *Will Mary's death bring England peace – or war?*

He didn't know any of the answers. All around him, silent snow began to fall.

When Kit returned to Seething Lane, Walsingham was still lying in his sickbed. Kit ran up the stairs to see him.

'It is all over now, Sir Francis,' Kit told him, and went on to describe Mary's execution, careful not to miss out a single detail. Walsingham was still too weak to talk much, but he managed a weary smile.

'I could not have done this without you, Kit,' he

said. 'Over these last few months, you have been my most faithful servant.'

'You do me great honour,' Kit replied. He wondered what his father would have said to this compliment, and to the circumstances that surrounded it. If he were still alive, would he even recognise his own son any more?

A week later Walsingham was up and about again, but he was still not well enough to leave the house.

'I heard from court today,' he told Kit one afternoon. 'The Queen is in a terrible rage.'

Kit was not at all surprised to hear this. Elizabeth's moods were as changeable as the tides.

'She denies she ever asked for Mary's execution, and is punishing everyone who was involved in it,' Walsingham explained.

'It is fortunate you are away from court, Sir Francis,' Kit observed.

'She is even accusing me of faking my illness,' Walsingham said. 'What do you say to this?' In his weakened state, the spymaster seemed to want reassurance from Kit.

'I think you have been very sick,' Kit replied. But

a seed of doubt was sown in his mind. Could it be that Walsingham had used his spymaster's cunning to exaggerate his illness and avoid the Queen's anger?

Whatever the answer, it was clear that Walsingham's health was now failing fast. His physician made frequent visits, and there was whispered talk of cancer. Despite this, the spymaster refused to rest. He worked harder than ever, and his secret Service continued to grow. He took on more agents to write and crack codes, and Kit spent many hours learning these skills from Thomas Phelippes. But the better Kit got at code breaking, the more trapped he felt. The death of Mary had not removed the Catholic threat as he had hoped – if anything, it had made it worse.

As Queen Elizabeth had feared, the reaction of Catholic countries to the execution of Mary Queen of Scots was serious. The year after Mary's death, in 1588, King Philip of Spain carried out his threat to send a flotilla of ships to invade England. Sir Francis and his agents worked flat out to provide naval intelligence that eventually led to the defeat of the Spanish Armada. It was possibly the spymaster's finest hour, but he received little credit for the English victory.

Long months dragged by and turned into years. Many things in Kit's life remained the same – he still spent much of his time sparring with Bess, who liked to tease him about his work.

'I've never met anyone lazier than you,' she would say. 'Call yourself a falconer's apprentice? I think I spend more time with those birds than you do.'

Kit would laugh this off by teasing her back.

'You're not much of a maid either,' he would say. 'Far too busy sticking your nose into other people's business. My room is in a filthy state – you can't have swept the floor for months.'

As time passed, Kit almost lost hope of leaving the Service. He resigned himself to a career as a code breaker, knowing that this was not without its risks. From what he had heard, very few code breakers ever died of natural causes.

But then one April morning in 1590, soon after his eighteenth birthday, everything changed. Kit was helping Walsingham sort out some papers in his study when he came across a pile of unpaid bills. He showed one of them to the spymaster.

'This bill is long overdue, Sir Francis,' Kit said.

Walsingham sighed. Illness and overwork had made their mark on the old man; he was now in his late fifties, with thinning white hair and a sallow complexion.

'Believe me, Kit, I am as poor as I am sick,' he said, peering at the bill.

'Nonsense!' exclaimed Kit. 'You work for the Queen!'

'True, but she has always taken my work for granted,' the spymaster replied, with some bitterness. 'She has never given me enough money to fund the Service that I run for her. Over the years, I have often paid my men from my own pocket – and that includes you, Kit.'

Kit thought of the hoard of silver coins he had earned since he began working for Walsingham, four years ago. It was stashed away under the floorboards of his room. To this day, Kit had never found a use for this small fortune.

'I have run out of money,' Walsingham said bluntly. 'I cannot pay any of my bills. I will die in debt, leaving nothing behind for my family.'

'Does the Queen know about this, Sir Francis?' Kit asked.

'If she does know, she doesn't care,' he replied. 'The truth is, she never forgave me for Mary's death, even though she now admits that it had to happen. These last few years, I have been out of the Queen's favour, even though she owes me both her life and the peace of her precious kingdom.'

This was the last conversation Kit ever had with Sir Francis. That night, the spymaster went to bed earlier than usual, complaining of severe stomach cramp. The next morning, he was dead.

CHAPTER 9

A strange calm descended on the house in Seething Lane, like a lull before a storm. Walsingham's spy network was a rudderless ship, drifting at sea and at the mercy of the elements.

Walsingham's wife and daughter arrived that morning to sort out the spymaster's personal affairs. For many years Sir Francis had kept Lady Ursula Walsingham and his only daughter Frances at arm's length, in ignorance of his secret working life. They had spent their time at Barn Elms, a manor house, which was a twenty-minute boat ride away down the Thames. Kit hardly knew these distinguished ladies, despite his years of working with Sir Francis. He tried to keep out of their way as they busied themselves with the practicalities that came with a death in the family.

'We shall have to hold the funeral tonight at St Paul's,' Kit overheard Lady Ursula say to her daughter. 'There is only enough money for a quiet and plain ceremony, under cover of darkness.'

She seemed more concerned with her financial situation than with the loss of her husband. Lady Ursula's face, lined with the wrinkles of old age, was pinched with worry.

'I had no idea that Father's affairs were in such a dreadful state,' replied Walsingham's daughter. 'How can this be, Mother?'

Lady Ursula shook her head.

'For that, you would have to ask the Queen herself,' she said angrily. 'He gave his whole life to that woman, and look what we have to show for it. A mountain of debt, nothing more.'

For all Kit's differences with Sir Francis, he was sorry to see things end in this way. He decided to go to St Paul's Cathedral that evening, to pay his respects to the late, great spymaster.

It was a chilly April night. As Kit stood in the cloisters outside St Paul's, he watched the torch-lit procession advance towards the tall stone church, bearing the lonely coffin of Sir Francis. Suddenly it dawned on Kit that Queen Elizabeth was not at the funeral, and she had not sent a single representative from court.

Sir Francis was right, he thought to himself. *She really couldn't care less about him.*

'It is good of the Queen to show her royal face,' said a sarcastic voice, echoing Kit's thoughts. Kit spun round to see his friend Thomas Phelippes standing behind him in the shadows.

'Like you, I came to bid farewell to Sir Francis,' said the code breaker. 'But I also came to give you a warning. I knew I'd find you here.'

'What do you mean, a warning?' asked Kit.

'You're in danger, Kit,' came the reply. 'Whoever takes the place of Sir Francis at court will need to bring in his own men, people he knows very well. He won't be able to trust Sir Francis' agents – and you know what happens to anyone in the Service who can't be trusted.'

It took a moment for this to sink in.

'What about you, Thomas?' Kit asked. 'Are you safe?'

Phelippes sniffed. 'I'm well known at court – don't forget, I was a witness at Mary's trial. They can't make someone like me just disappear. But as for you…'

Phelippes didn't need to finish his sentence.

A familiar panic rose up in Kit, the sense that things were spiralling out of control.

'What should I do?' he asked.

'Now's your chance to run,' Phelippes replied. 'Tomorrow may be too late.'

Kit grasped his friend's arm.

'Thank you so much, Thomas,' he said. 'In this world of treachery, you are one of the few people I can trust.'

Keeping out of sight, Kit hurried out of the churchyard. But his way out through Saint Paul's gates was barred by two smartly dressed men, deep in whispered conversation.

'Are you coming back to Seething Lane with me tonight, Lord Essex?' one of them asked. 'I need your help to go through all those papers.'

'Of course, Sir Robert,' the other replied.

Kit recognised these names; he had often heard Walsingham mention them in scathing tones. Sir Robert was the son of Sir William Cecil, Lord Treasurer and perhaps the most powerful of the Queen's advisors. Thanks to his connections at court, Sir Robert must be tipped to take over from Sir

Francis. But Lord Essex, one of the Queen's favourite courtiers, probably had other ideas.

Kit hid behind a pillar to listen. The men's lowered voices were only just audible.

'Sir Francis kept all his secret files at his London town house,' said Lord Essex. 'I understand that he never showed them to anyone.'

'I need the names of everyone who worked for Sir Francis,' said Sir Robert. 'The evidence must be hidden in that house.'

'Sir Francis had a private study there,' suggested Lord Essex. 'I'll wager that's where you'll find what you're looking for.'

The two men walked out onto the street, where a horse and carriage awaited them.

'Seething Lane,' Sir Robert said to the driver, climbing in. Then they disappeared into the night.

Kit stood alone in St Paul's Churchyard, his heart pounding.

Thomas was right, he thought. *It's only a matter of time before they discover who I am, if they don't already know.*

Suddenly, two hands grabbed him from behind. Kit wheeled around, and grabbed the wrists of his assailant.

'Get off! You're hurting me!' cried a girl's voice. It was Bess.

Kit staggered backwards, so surprised he could hardly speak.

'What are you doing here?' he asked.

'I'm trying to help you!' said Bess, rubbing her wrists. 'Is this all the thanks I get?'

Kit stared at her, astonished.

'How can you possibly help me?' he said.

Bess looked down, embarrassed.

'I know all about what you do, Kit,' she whispered. 'I've known for years.'

'But how the devil…' began Kit.

'I have eyes and ears in my head,' Bess interrupted. 'There had to be some reason why you were so close to Sir Francis, and why you were always out on some errand for him. I just put two and two together.'

'Why didn't you ever say anything to me?' asked Kit.

'I didn't want to make things difficult for you,' she replied. 'And I knew that whatever you were doing, it had to be secret. You didn't want someone like me getting in the way.'

Kit was at a loss for words.

'I know you so well, Kit, and it's obvious you're

not happy in your work,' Bess continued. 'You were a different person when we grew up together. Now that Sir Francis has passed away, it's your chance to start all over again.'

She dropped a big canvas satchel on the ground. There was a jingling sound.

'My money!' gasped Kit. 'How did you find it?'

'As I said, I'm not blind…and unfortunately for me, it's my job to sweep your room,' Bess said, smiling. 'When I left Seething Lane tonight, the house was crawling with strangers trying to search the place. I thought I'd better bring this with me.'

Kit sighed.

'I have always underestimated you, Bess,' he said. 'You're brighter than you look.'

Bess punched him playfully in the chest.

'Listen, stupid, you need to get away from here before those people catch up with you,' she said. Her delight at outsmarting him was infuriating.

'Where shall I go?' he asked. He was in her hands; she seemed to have thought of everything.

'Follow me,' she replied. 'I haven't got time to explain now. But you can carry this bag for me. It's very heavy!'

Kit and Bess ran down the sloping streets towards the river, heading east towards Tower Dock. Bess stopped for a moment to catch her breath.

'Do you remember my older brother Will?' she asked.

Kit nodded. 'He ran away to sea just before my father died.'

'That's right. Well, his ship is in dock on the Thames tonight, at Galley Quay.'

Suddenly Kit understood what Bess was up to.

'Do you think he'd stow me away on board his ship?' he asked.

'He might, if you made it worth his while,' Bess replied, glancing at the satchel. 'Which I think you probably could.'

'Where is he bound for on his next voyage?' asked Kit.

'The New World,' replied Bess. 'His captain is taking one of the new trade routes to Virginia in America.'

Kit had always wondered what this land of discovery was like, thousands of miles away on the other side of the world. Perhaps he was destined to find out.

Kit and Bess arrived at Galley Quay, a busy dock not far from the Tower. Will's trading ship was being loaded with a few last crates of provisions, ready for its long journey across the ocean. Bess beckoned to her brother, who came over to talk with her. He had a friendly, open face like his sister. Kit knew at once that he could be trusted.

'Bess told me all about you,' Will said to Kit with a knowing smile. 'I understand you want to disappear. How much can you pay me for this favour? It could cost me my livelihood, so it had better be worth it.'

Kit handed Will his satchel.

'If you can stow me on board your ship tonight, all this will be yours to share with Bess,' he replied.

Will opened the bag and whistled at its contents. Bess looked at Kit.

'Are you sure about this?' she asked. 'Don't you want to keep some money for yourself?'

But Kit knew what he really wanted, more than anything else in the world. He had never felt more certain.

'Come with me, Bess,' he said. 'I don't need that money – in fact, I never want to see it again. But I do need you.'

'You want me to run away with you?' Bess gasped, wide-eyed. Her brother laughed.

'It's about time you did something adventurous with your life, Bess,' he said. 'You can't stay in that dingy house in Seething Lane forever. Besides, I know of a perfect place to stow you both away.'

Bess laughed.

'How could I possibly refuse such an offer?' she said, her eyes shining with excitement. She grabbed Kit's hand, and together they followed Will onto his ship.

As Kit hid with Bess among the cargo, deep in the hold of the ship, he had to pinch himself to make sure he was awake. He could not remember the last time he had felt so full of hope.

God only knows what the future has in store for me, he thought. *But I'm free at last. I'm one step ahead of the enemy, just as Sir Francis always told me to be. And with Bess for company, I won't be alone anymore.*

The next morning at sunrise, the ship raised anchor and set sail for the New World. High overhead, two hawks hovered for a while, then flew out of sight.